D0110104

CONTENTS

THE CHARACTERS

Siddhartha Gautama, Lord Buddha

Siddhartha, the heir to the throne of Kapilavastu, is disenchanted and aimless. Leaving his palace, wife and child behind, what will he discover about life and death?

Suddhodana and Mahamaya

Siddhartha's parents always knew that their son was destined for greatness, but how will Mahamaya's dream and Suddhodana's expectations turn out?

Yashodhara and Rahula

Siddhartha's wife and baby son are left as Yashodhara's husband sets off for the wilderness to explore the greatest truths of life. Will they ever see him again?

SIDDHARTHA GAUTAMA

THE LIFE OF THE BUDDHA

based on original sources

www.realreads.co.uk

Retold by R.N. Pillai
Illustrated by Aniruddha Mukherjee

Published by Real Reads Ltd
Stroud, Gloucestershire, UK
www.realreads.co.uk

Text copyright © DC Books, 2013
Illustrations copyright © DC Books, 2013
Published in conjunction with DC Books, Kottayam, Kerala, India

First published in 2013

ISBN 978-1-906230-61-6

Printed in China by Wai Man Book Binding (China) Ltd
Designed by Lucy Guenot
Typeset by Bookcraft Ltd, Stroud, Gloucestershire

Ananda

The Buddha's cousin and constant attendant, Ananda loves the Buddha as no one else does. He remembers Buddha's every word. What use will he make of his gift?

Mahamoggallana and Sariputta

Buddha's chief disciples are second only to him in wisdom, but what they have to learn from their master's teachings will follow quite different paths.

Anathapindika

This rich merchant gives everything away for the sake of the Buddha and his teachings. Will he ever become rich again?

Devadatta and Angulimala

Seduced by selfishness and violence, Devadatta and Angulimala find it hard to understand the Buddha's message. What will they learn?

SIDDHARTHA GAUTAMA

Two thousand six hundred years ago a wise and compassionate king, Suddhodana, ruled over the kingdom of Sakya on the Himalayan slopes of northern India. Suddhodana's chief queen was the virtuous and charitable Mahamaya.

One full moon night, as Queen Mahamaya lay asleep, she had a beautiful dream. She felt she was being carried away by *devas*, residents of heaven, to a sacred lake in the Himalayas. There she was bathed and dressed in heavenly clothes. A white elephant carrying a silver lotus flower in its trunk walked around her three times before entering her womb.

When the king heard about the dream he invited sixty-four brahmin astrologers to interpret it. 'Your Majesty,' they told him, 'you shall beget a son who will forsake the kingdom for the sake of ultimate wisdom. He will bring deliverance to all mankind.'

When her time came, according to custom, Queen Mahamaya set out to deliver the child in her parental home. King Suddhodana made arrangements for her royal procession to the house of the Koliyas, her own clan. As they reached a beautiful spot called the Lumbini Garden, the queen went into labour and asked the palanquin bearers to set her down. The curtains were drawn around her on all sides, and as she stood under a *sala* tree holding one of its branches, she was painlessly delivered of a baby boy. The baby's body glowed in divine splendour. He stood up and took seven steps forwards. At each step, a lotus flower sprang up to support his feet.

'I am the chief of all worlds,' announced the baby. 'I have no equal. I am supreme. This is my final incarnation.' It was full moon day in the late spring month of Vaisakha, which in the Christian calendar was May of the year 566 BCE.

There was great rejoicing in the royal household at the birth of a son to the king.

News spread throughout the kingdom that a divine child had been born to King Suddhodana and Queen Mahamaya. Asita, a venerable sage, came to the palace to see the blessed child. He took up the child in his arms and started to weep.

A worried Suddhodana asked Asita, 'Is anything wrong with the baby?'

'No, on the contrary,' replied Asita. 'Your baby will be an all-enlightened Buddha who will preach the ultimate truth to humankind. Sadly I won't have the good fortune to hear him as I shall have passed away by then. I am sorry for myself. That is why I weep.'

For the naming ceremony, King Suddhodana invited eight brahmin astrologers. Seven of them predicted that two destinies were open to the child. 'If he chooses to govern,' they told the king, 'he will be a sceptre-wielding *loka chakravarti*, an emperor of the world. But should he take the spiritual path, he will be a *dharmic chakaravarti*, a spiritual emperor, revealing to humanity the ultimate goal of their existence. And how will his path be chosen? If he encounters four unhappy things – an old man, a sick man, a dead body, and a monk – he is sure to turn away from the worldly life.'

The eighth astrologer, Kondanna, an eighteen-year-old brahmin, said with certainty, 'This baby will be none other than a Buddha.'

The astrologers named the child Siddhartha, meaning 'the wish-fulfilled one'.

Sadly, Queen Mahamaya passed away just seven days after giving birth to Siddhartha. Prajapati Gotami, another of Suddhodana's wives, took charge of Siddhartha, handing over her own son Nanda to the care of a nurse.

Each year King Suddhodana marked the beginning of the annual ploughing season by ploughing a field with a golden plough. As this took place soon after Siddhartha's birth, he left the baby in the care of nurses, and stepped into the field and took his place behind the plough. As the festivities began, the nurses left the child at the foot of a rose apple tree and went to watch. When they returned, an amazing sight met their eyes – the child was sitting in the lotus position, or *padmasana*, in deep meditation. The shadow of the rose apple tree, rather than moving as the sun moved, had stayed in the same place all the time the child was meditating, protecting him from the sun's hot rays. On hearing this the king, seeing the miracle, bowed before the divine child in great reverence.

As Siddhartha grew up he excelled in academic and martial arts. The young prince was charming and affectionate, and lacked nothing by way of comfort.

King Suddhodana took particular care
to ensure that his son did not have any
opportunity to hear about or feel suffering of
any kind. Three beautiful palaces were built
specifically for Siddhartha to live in, one for
each season, with high walls that shielded him
from the outside world.

Prince Siddhartha Gautama was
compassionate towards all living beings. One
day while he was walking in the woods, his
cousin Devadatta took his bow and arrow and
shot down a swan that was flying overhead.
Both of them ran towards the fallen bird;
Siddhartha reached it first, and took hold of
the wounded bird which was struggling for
life. He gently pulled out the arrow, applied
healing herbs to the wound, and stroked the
frightened bird.

'Give the bird to me,' Devadatta demanded
angrily. 'I shot it down.'

Siddhartha refused. 'Had you killed the swan,' he told his cousin, 'it would have been yours. I have saved its life, therefore it belongs to me. Let us go to the court of wise men and ask them to decide.'

The court of wise men gave instant judgment – 'A life belongs to one who saves it, not to one who tries to destroy it.'

Despite living a life of luxury and being protected from the harsh realities of the world, Siddhartha always appeared to be lost in thought. This worried King Suddhodana, who lived in constant fear of the astrologers' prediction coming true. 'What will happen if my son chooses to leave everything behind and seek the spiritual path? There will be no heir to the throne.'

The king did everything in his power to distract the pensive Siddhartha. The palace was filled with music and dance, and a festive air was maintained throughout each day. 'I forbid you to talk about anything unpleasant in the prince's presence,' the king instructed his courtiers. But Siddhartha was still preoccupied.

'Get him married,' the wise men advised Suddhodana. All the beautiful maidens from the region were invited to the palace in the hope that Siddhartha would choose one of them to be his wife. The prince offered valuable presents to all those who came, but specially favoured a girl called Yashodhara. She belonged to the

Koliya clan, and was Suddhodana's niece and
Devadatta's sister.

The royal wedding between Siddhartha
and Yashodhara was celebrated across the
kingdom. Now Suddhodana was at peace – the
young couple seemed very much in love. But
Prince Siddhartha was still strangely disturbed.

'The high walls around the palace will
shield my son from the outside world,'
Suddhodana kept telling himself.

One day Siddhartha asked Suddhodana, 'Father, may I go out and take a look at how the people in our kingdom live?'

'Very well, my son,' his father replied. 'You may, but only after I have made all the necessary arrangements.'

The king arranged for flags and bunting to be put up all along the route, and ensured that no unseemly sights appeared before his son.

The prince stepped up into the chariot driven by Channa, a faithful charioteer of the royal household, and they drove away. Suddenly in front of them appeared a toothless old man with

sunken eyes and silvery hair. He was dressed in dirty rags, and walked unsteadily, supported by a stick. The prince saw the old man, but did not know what to make of what he was seeing.

'What is that, Channa?' he asked.

'It is old age, which will ultimately befall everyone,' Channa explained.

The prince was unhappy with what he had seen, and ordered Channa to drive home. Siddhartha now knew that one day he too would grow old, and would be grey, toothless and wrinkled.

'Is there no escape from old age?' the prince asked himself.

The prince wanted to see more, so he asked his father to allow him to venture into the city of Kapilavastu. Reluctantly, Suddhodana agreed. Dressed as an ordinary man and again accompanied by Channa, he walked the city streets, where he saw blacksmiths, goldsmiths, dyers and bakers at work.

Suddenly, as if from nowhere, a man came into view lying on the ground rolling around in pain, twisting his body, holding his stomach with both hands, and crying in agony. There were purple patches all over his body, and he was gasping for breath.

The kind and compassionate prince stepped down from the chariot, knelt beside the man, and laid his head on his lap.

'Channa, tell me, what is the matter with this man?'

'O prince,' replied Channa, 'he is suffering from the plague. His body is burning all over. Please do not touch him, as you may also become infected.'

Siddhartha realised that there must be many hundreds who, like this man, were suffering from unbearably painful diseases. He returned to the palace with a heavy heart.

Siddhartha was now determined to find out more about life outside the palace. Disguised as a youth from a noble family, he yet again set out to see the city with Channa. An unfamiliar sight caught his attention. He saw four men carrying a plank on which was a frail body, which was lying quite still. Wailing men and women followed the body, which was set down on a pile of wood. Both wood and body were then set on fire.

'What is this, Channa?' asked the prince. 'Why does that man allow himself to be burnt?'

'He is dead, Prince Siddhartha.'

'Will everyone die? Is this what death looks like?'

'Every living being has to die,' replied Channa. 'There is no escape for anyone.'

Shocked and bewildered, Siddhartha hastened back to the palace. He found it hard to understand that death was unpreventable. 'Surely there must be a way to put an end to death,' he thought to himself. 'I must find out how.'

When the prince went to the city for the fourth time, he saw a shaven-headed monk with a peaceful and inspiring countenance. The monk was wearing orange robes.

'Who is he, Channa?' asked Siddhartha.

'He is a monk,' answered Channa. 'He lives in a temple and supports himself with alms, instructing people in moral and religious life.'

The prince sighed with relief. 'Yes, I will be a monk like him,' he said to himself as he returned to the palace.

Sitting in the garden later that day, Siddhartha received news that his wife had delivered a baby boy, their first child. The boy was named Rahula, meaning an obligation, or a bond.

Siddhartha was concerned that however hard people tried to live full and rewarding lives, all their efforts led only to the grave. He felt terrified by the prospect of death. 'Is there no way out?' he asked himself. 'Will everything perish? There must be another way.' He was gradually making up his mind to make his life's mission to seek out the alternative to death, to search for immortality – if immortality did indeed exist.

It was now time for him to leave behind the pleasures of the palace. Siddhartha asked Channa to get his favourite horse Kanthaka ready. In the middle of the night, as he was about to leave, he stopped to take one last look at his wife and new-born son. He stood on the threshold and cast a glance at the sleeping mother and child. He had an urge to kiss his son, but feared that it would awaken his wife.

'However hard it is to leave,' Siddhartha reminded himself, 'love for one's wife and child is nothing compared with love for all humanity.'

Siddhartha rode off into the darkness, accompanied only by the faithful Channa. When they reached the River Anoma at the border with the neighbouring kingdom of Magadha the prince dismounted, removed all his jewellery and princely garments, and handed them to Channa.

'Take these and ride back to my father on Kanthaka,' he told Channa. 'Tell him that I am going to find out if there is a way to overcome old age, disease and death. If I discover it I shall return and teach you all.'

As he turned to walk on alone, Kanthaka refused to move. 'Kanthaka, go with Channa. Do not wait for me,' said Siddhartha, gently patting his horse. Tears rolled down Kanthaka's cheeks. Fixing its gaze on his master, it fell down dead, overcome by the pain of separation.

After Channa had left, Siddhartha shaved his head, changed into monk's robes, and set out.

On his wanderings Siddhartha came to the city of Rajagriha, where Bimbisara, the wise and devout king of Magadha, lived. Reports reached Bimbisara that a most handsome young man was roaming his kingdom with a begging bowl.

Bimbisara, deeply spiritual by nature, went to meet him. He was so impressed that he offered his daughter's hand and half his kingdom to Siddhartha. Siddhartha gently declined. 'I am on a spiritual quest seeking a solution to all human suffering,' he told the king. 'I cannot stay. I will return when I have found the answer.'

Hearing that Siddhartha had set out on his spiritual mission, five of his friends also left home and travelled to join him. One of them was Kondanna, who had predicted that Siddhartha would be none other than a Buddha.

They all became disciples of a great religious teacher called Alara Kalama. Alara Kalama taught them a form of meditation called *samatha* to calm the mind and free it from inner turmoil. Siddhartha mastered the technique easily, and quickly rose to the seventh level.

'This tremendous joy that you experience in the seventh stage will be with you even after death,' Alara Kalama told his disciples.

'But have you nothing more to teach?' a dissatisfied Siddhartha asked the teacher. 'There are still so many things which are unclear and unexplained. I must have an answer to old age, sickness and death.'

'I have taught you all I know,' replied Alara Kalama. 'You are now my equal. If you are not satisfied you must go to Uddaka, the son of Rama, who will teach you the eighth and last stage of *samatha* meditation.'

Siddhartha and his friends left Alara Kalama and walked through the woods of Maghada until they found Uddaka Ramputta. Under his guidance Siddhartha soared to the eighth stage of *samatha* meditation. Uddaka was amazed.

'You are now my equal,' he said. 'You must stay here as a teacher.'

'But old age, sickness and death – how are they to be overcome?' asked Siddhartha.

'I do not have an answer to that,' replied Uddaka. 'I am only a teacher after all. But the level of *samatha* meditation that you have now achieved will remain with you even after death.'

Siddhartha and his five friends bade farewell to Uddaka and continued their journey.

At that time in India, many people believed that one way of discovering ultimate truth was to test the body by going without food and living with as little as possible. Inspired by this belief, Siddhartha and his friends started fasting, and meditating in the open air whatever the weather.

Siddhartha gradually reduced the amount of food he ate, at first living on roots of plants, leaves and fruit, and finally on nothing but cow dung. He became so emaciated that his legs looked like bamboo poles, his backbone like a rope, his chest like a collapsed roof, and his eyes sunk into their sockets. When he meditated he held his breath for so long that he was often overcome by terrible pain. Wearing only rags, he meditated in the hot summer sun and the bitter cold of winter.

For six long years he tortured himself in this way, but still did not find any answers. One day he fainted from sheer exhaustion, and would have died if a shepherd had not given him a little milk. Having been so close to death and still without any new understanding, he decided that starvation was not the answer – he needed to eat enough food to stay alive.

When his five friends saw that Siddhartha had started eating again they left him in disgust, accusing him of leading a luxurious life. But Siddhartha had discovered something very important – that there was a way to live which meant neither giving up worldly comforts entirely nor becoming self-indulgent. It was possible to choose a middle path, or *madhyama marga*.

In the nearby village of Senani lived a beautiful and rich girl named Sujata. One morning she was getting ready to make a prayerful offering to the tree god. She sent her maid to sweep and clean the foot of the banyan tree near the River Neranjara.

When the maid returned she was very excited. She told Sujata, 'The tree god has come in person to receive your offering. He is sitting under the tree meditating.'

Sujata was now excited too, and their joy knew no bounds when they saw a young figure sitting in meditation – surely a god come in answer to their prayers. It was of course Siddhartha, who graciously accepted the offering of sweet milk porridge before crossing the river on his way towards Gaya.

When he reached Gaya, Siddhartha looked
for a suitable place to meditate. He chose
the foot of a large banyan tree. With his face
turned towards the east, he began meditating,
determined not to stir until he had discovered
the highest wisdom, supreme enlightenment.
Here he practised a way of meditating called
anapana sati or 'awareness of breathing',
concentrating as fully as possible on each
inbreath and outbreath.

While Siddhartha was meditating, a tempter
called Mara came to seduce him by reminding
him of all the pleasures he had chosen to give
up. Mara appeared before Siddhartha with
a huge army and started to attack him, but
their arrows turned into flowers and fell at
Siddhartha's feet. Mara then tried to tempt
Siddhartha with his three beautiful daughters,
but Siddhartha remained undaunted – firm,
brave and steadfast in his endeavour.

It was again full moon night in the month of Vaisakha, the month in which Siddhartha had been born. He was now thirty-five years old. As he meditated on this auspicious night, Siddhartha's sharpened mind started penetrating the realms of reality. He began seeing his past lives. He had been born as a god many times, he had been kings and emperors, his incarnations numbered millions upon millions.

He continued to meditate, and as the night went on he began to understand the truth about the cycle of life and death, how things never really end and start but come around again and again. Everything a person does in their life, both the good things and the bad things, have an effect on what will happen in their next life. Everything has a reason, everything has a result – this is the cycle of *karma*.

It was now that part of the night which comes just before dawn, and Siddhartha understood to the core of his being how everything in the world is connected with everything else. Nothing exists independently, in isolation. Nothing can be ignored, nothing can be left out, nothing is unimportant.

By the time morning came Siddhartha had become the Buddha, which means 'the enlightened one'. He knew the ultimate truth. He was the source of supreme wisdom. He had solved the riddle of life, discovered the cause of sorrow, and found the answer to old age, sickness and death. From this time on he would become known as the Lord Buddha, and the banyan tree where he found enlightenment, or *bodhi*, became known as the Bodhi Tree.

The Lord Buddha remained under the Bodhi Tree in Gaya for another seven weeks, enjoying the bliss of his new-found freedom. In the fourth week he created a beautiful jewelled chamber to meditate in.

One day it started raining, and a huge king cobra appeared from the forest and wound its coils into a cushion for the Buddha to sit on. The snake sheltered the Buddha's head from the rain with its hood. When the rain stopped, the cobra turned into a beautiful young man who paid his respects to the Buddha. He was a god come from heaven.

On the fiftieth morning, two merchants called Tapussa and Bhallika came. They offered the Buddha rice cakes and honey. The Buddha plucked a few strands of hair from his head and gave it to them as a gift. These strands of hair, called *kesadhathu*, are preserved even now in the famous Shwedagon Pagoda.

Towards the end of his time under the Bodhi Tree, the high god Brahma Sahampati appeared and implored the Buddha to preach the doctrine he had discovered, the principles or *dharma* underlying the order of the universe, so that everyone could benefit from it.

The Lord Buddha decided that he would start by instructing the five friends who had set out on the path of discovery with him. They now lived in the city of Kasi, so Buddha went to find them there.

'Look,' they said when they saw him approaching, 'Siddhartha is coming, that lover of luxury. Just ignore him.' But as the Buddha drew nearer they could immediately see that this was not the same old Siddhartha, but a divine being from whose body rays of colour emanated. The monks took his bowl and robe and laid them down gently; they prepared a seat for him, and one of them hurried off to fetch water to wash the Buddha's feet.

The Lord Buddha took his seat, and began to tell them what he now understood. 'I have discovered the path to that peaceful state of mind called *nirvana*, beyond all pain and death. It is a state of happiness beyond description.'

The five monks were sceptical. 'Friend Siddhartha, how did you attain *nirvana* from living a life of ease and comfort, when you could not achieve it through hardship and penance?'

'I am no longer your friend, nor am I a human being or a god. You now see before you the Buddha, the *tathagata*, the one beyond all earthly comings and goings. And believe me,' he continued, 'I have not lived a life of ease and comfort. By taking the middle path, avoiding self-indulgence on the one hand and self-mortification on the other, I have arrived at the ultimate truth. If you follow my instructions, you too will find *nirvana*.'

The Buddha then explained to the monks the four noble truths which form the foundation of Buddhism.

The first noble truth is that everyone must experience suffering and pain at some point in their lives, including the inevitable sufferings of illness, aging and death. But because we all experience pain, it is something to learn from and be positive about.

The second noble truth is that sorrow and spiritual pain come from expectation and desire, again feelings shared by everyone which we can all learn from.

The third noble truth is that pain and sorrow can be overcome by understanding what they mean.

The fourth noble truth is that sorrow and spiritual pain do not last forever. There are things we can do in our lives to overcome them.

The five monks listened attentively to what Lord Buddha told them. 'So what must we do to overcome sorrow?' one of them asked.

The Lord Buddha then explained what he had learned about the middle way, and told his friends about 'the eightfold path' to eliminate suffering. He told them about the eight ways to understand how the order of things works, and encouraged them to meditate on each one so they could understand for themselves what each of them meant.

Each part of the eightfold path starts with the word 'right', which Lord Buddha explained means 'perfect' or 'ideal', something to work towards.

The first of the eight is right perspective, learning to see the world as it really is rather than how we or other people would like it to be. The second is right intention, or doing things for good, well-thought-out reasons.

The third is right speech, or choosing carefully what we say. The fourth is right conduct, not acting in ways that are harmful to ourselves or to others.

The fifth is right livelihood, not engaging in harmful trades or occupations, while the sixth is right endeavour, doing things in a considered, thoughtful way.

The seventh is right attention, keeping our minds on whatever it is we are doing, and the eighth is right concentration, giving everything necessary to the task in hand.

Finally, Lord Buddha showed the monks how he had learned to meditate, using the awareness of his breathing to keep him focused on the transience of the universe. He called this way of meditating *vipassana* or 'mindfulness of breath'.

By the time Lord Buddha had finished explaining the Buddhist way to the five monks, they knew in the core of their being that this was true enlightenment, and became Lord Buddha's first followers.

The Buddha now started to travel far and wide, and many disciples joined the Buddhist community, or *sangha*. Siddhartha's father, King Suddhodana, heard of the Buddha's teachings, and requested that his son pay a visit to the palace at Kapilavasthu, the home that he left in search of spiritual truth.

Yashodhara set eyes on the husband who had abandoned her seven years ago. She realised that this was no longer Prince Siddhartha, but the enlightened Buddha, who had found the ultimate truth. She turned to her and Siddhartha's son. 'Rahula, this is your father. Ask him for your inheritance,' she said. The Buddha had no material wealth to give, but accepted Rahula into the *sangha* as a monk.

At that time the caste system, by which Indian society was rigidly divided into higher and lower social orders, was the way most Indians thought people's status was ordained. The Buddha did not believe in caste distinction, and men and women from all levels of society became his followers. Upali, the great Buddhist monk, was originally the palace barber; another disciple, Sunita, came from a poor family which gathered dead flowers from shrines.

Buddha's personal attendant, who served him with utmost devotion, was his cousin Ananda. The Buddha's two chief disciples, Sariputta and Mahamoggallana, were both young brahmins. While the pure Sariputta had followed a spiritual path since he was a boy, Mahamoggallana – who had great supernatural powers and was said to be able to speak with the dead and fly through the air – had a more chequered past, as the circumstances of his death were to prove.

While he was travelling in Magadha, Mahamoggallana was set upon by robbers and killed in a brutal fashion. When asked why Mahamoggallana had not protected and saved himself, Buddha explained that Mahamoggallana had murdered his parents in a previous life, so had no escape from reaping the consequences.

One of the Buddha's most ardent followers was Anathapindika, the wealthiest merchant in Kosala. As well as being one of the Buddha's most devout followers, Anathapindika became renowned for his generosity towards the Buddhist *sangha*, giving the monks food and shelter; sometimes there were as many as a hundred monks staying in his house.

Even this was not enough generosity for Anathapindika. He decided that he would buy the pleasure garden belonging to Prince Jeta and donate it to Buddha for a monastery.

'What is the price of your garden?' he asked the prince.

'The price? Fill the entire garden with gold, that is the price,' replied Jeta haughtily, never expecting Anathapindika to take him seriously.

Jeta was stunned when he saw Anathapindika bringing cartloads of gold coins to cover the ground. Touched by the merchant's devotion, the prince donated the garden to the *sangha* for free.

The Lord Buddha did not let Anathapindika's generosity go unrewarded. The night before he died, Anathapindika visited Buddha at the Jeta monastery, as he did several times each day. Lord Buddha blessed him, and told him he would be remembered as long as any god.

Not everyone understood Lord Buddha's
teachings of right intention and right conduct.
One notable exception was Devadatta, the
Buddha's own cousin and brother-in-law.
Devadatta had joined the *sangha* and made
some progress, but greed, hatred and delusion
poisoned his mind.

King Bimbisara of Magadha had been
one of Siddhartha's earliest supporters, but
his son Ajatasatru was jealous and devious.
With Devadatta's encouragement, Ajatasatru
persuaded King Bimbisara to abdicate. Not
content with his new position as king, Ajatasatru
imprisoned his father and starved him to death.

Devadatta's evil machinations did not stop
there. He convinced Ajatasatru to set Nalagiri,
the royal elephant, on the Buddha. Nalagiri
charged towards Buddha, but fell at his feet,
subdued by his benevolence. Next Devadatta
sent archers to assassinate the Buddha, but

they were so influenced by his teachings that they became disciples. Finally, the boulder that Devadatta sent hurtling down to crush the Buddha merely scratched the great teacher's toe.

In the end Devadatta was repentant of his misdeeds, and journeyed to where the Buddha was, to apologise. As he arrived at the monastery, the earth opened up and swallowed him.

Another notable repentant was the notorious robber who came to be known as Angulimala or 'garland of fingers'. He was the son of the chaplain to the king of Kosala – he was clever and prone to getting into trouble. When he was born his father named him Ahimsaka, meaning 'the harmless one', but that didn't save him.

He was sent to study under a well-known guru, but the other students grew jealous of Ahimsaka's speedy progress and sought to turn his master against him.

The guru told Ahimsaka that his training was now complete, but as the traditional final gift always given by a student to a guru, the teacher said he must bring him a thousand fingers, each taken from a different victim, thinking that his unruly student would surely be killed in the course of seeking this grisly prize.

Ahimsaka moved into the jungle, where he would fall upon unwary travellers, kill them, and cut off their fingers. He then strung the fingers together into a garland or *mala,* which he wore round his neck. This was when everyone started calling him Angulimala.

Eventually Angulimala needed just one more finger to complete his garland for the guru, but by this time the king's army was close to capturing him. Fearing for her son's life, Angulimala's mother ran into the jungle one moonlit night to warn him of the impending danger. 'Here comes my last victim,' Angulimala thought.

Angulimala positioned himself, axe in hand, ready for the final act. But Lord Buddha saw what was about to happen, and materialised in place of Angulimala's mother. All night long Angulimala stalked the Buddha, axe in hand, but whenever he seemed to be close enough to strike, his intended victim would reappear in the distance. When it was almost daybreak an exasperated Angulimala shouted, 'Stop!'

Without turning, Lord Buddha uttered calmly, 'I *have* stopped, but you haven't. I have stopped killing living beings, but you have yet to learn that.' At that moment the Buddha turned to look at Angulimala, and the robber fell to the ground, his sword flying from his hand.

The next morning, when the king visited the Buddha's monastery, he was surprised to see a reformed Angulimala in monk's yellow robes. As the bandit had already become a monk, the king spared his life.

When Angulimala went around begging for alms, people who had lost their relatives at his hands threw stones at him, and he would return to the monastery bleeding and bruised. The Buddha comforted him. 'It is better to receive punishment here and now than to suffer in hell, which is where you would have gone for the horrible crimes you committed.'

Lord Buddha and his followers never forgot that the search for the middle way had started with the important question of why we all have to suffer and die, and it was not surprising that these were the subjects which came up again and again in his teachings.

To anyone who asked him, Buddha would explain that though we must all pass through the cycle of being born, getting older, and eventually dying, this is a natural process which reminds us of how we should value and cherish life.

Death, he told his followers, is not the end of life, it is merely the end of the body we inhabit in this life. Life is like water in a stream – just because the water has passed by does not mean the stream has ceased to exist.

Lord Buddha explained how the fear of death stems from the fear of losing our identity and place in the world. We know that we shall die long before we do – this helps us to understand that everything is changing all the time, and how important it is to value what we have right now.

One day a woman called Kisa Gautami came to the Buddha carrying her dead child. She was desperate, and pleaded with the Buddha. 'Please use your divine powers and bring my child back to life.'

The Buddha spoke to her calmly. 'Bring me some mustard seeds from a house where no one has ever died,' he told her.

Kisa Gautami went from door to door throughout the neighbourhood, asking for mustard seeds, but she could not find a single house where no one had ever died.

Kisa Gautami now understood what the great teacher was saying, and returned to the Buddha serenely contemplating the universality of death. She joined the women's monastery, and at her own death attained *nirvana*.

Another important subject that Buddha was always being asked by his followers was the true nature of *karma*, the understanding that everything a person does in their life has an effect on what will happen in their next life.

'Do we have any influence over what becomes our own *karma*?' asked one disciple.

'Indeed you do,' replied Buddha. 'Think of *karma* as something you choose to do, rather than something that happens to you. *Karma* can only result from deliberate action; if there is no will or intention there can be no *karma*.'

'So what sort of actions are involved in creating *karma*?' asked the disciple.

'*Karma* can be created by body, mind and speech,' explained Buddha. 'Harming another living being, stealing, lying, speaking harsh words, greed and anger will all result in bad *karma*. Kindness, consideration, generosity, thoughtfulness – all will result in good *karma*.'

The Buddha's followers sometimes found it hard to understand his lofty ideas, so he often explained them using simple stories.

To explain the importance of right intention, he told a story about a beggar woman who bought a small oil lamp and placed it with great devotion in front of Buddha's monastery. The tiny lamp looked so ridiculous that a senior monk wanted to put it out. He tried his best to extinguish the flame, but failed. Lord Buddha happened to pass by, and said to the monk, 'The intention behind the action of leaving that lamp was so pure and so strong that you would not be able to put the flame out even with all the waters of the four oceans.'

In another example of right intention, Buddha told the story of Velama, a brahmin, who had given away hundreds of gifts – bowls of gold and silver filled with jewels, horses with trappings, embroidered coverlets, crimson cushions, and fine lengths of cloth. When he died, he found that he had not been transported to highest heaven, and could not understand why. 'The reason,' said the Buddha, 'is that Velama had distributed his gifts to the undeserving. Had Velama donated just one or two of his gifts to someone who was spiritually worthy of them then he would have been transported to the highest heaven.'

To illustrate right endeavour and right conduct the Buddha told of some little boys who were playing on a muddy road when Lord Buddha passed by with his alms bowl. Seeing the Lord, one of the boys collected a heap of sand in his cupped palms and emptied it into the bowl, as he did so imagining that he was donating gold. As a result of this simple but heartfelt gift, the boy was reborn a prince.

The Buddha was now nearing his eightieth year, and was growing physically weak. He confided in Ananda, his constant attendant, that he had decided that he would pass away within three months.

Together with Ananda, Buddha started journeying through the countryside, instructing people in *dharma* wherever he visited. At last he arrived at a place called Pava. One of Buddha's wealthy devotees, Chunda, invited the Buddha and monks to join him for their noon meal. The elaborate spread included a delicacy called *sukaramaddava*, made with truffles.

Buddha drew Chunda to one side, and said quietly to him, 'Chunda, I would like you to serve the *sukaramaddava* only to me.'

'So be it, Lord,' replied Chunda. As he had been bidden, he served the delicacy to the master, but not to any of the other monks.

Buddha called Chunda to one side again. 'Chunda, I would like you to bury all the remaining *sukaramaddava* in a deep hole in the ground. It should be eaten only by a master, and not by any other living being.' Again Chunda did as he had been asked.

Lord Buddha had chosen that his death be brought about by eating the *sukaramaddava*, which he knew was poisonous, and he knew that he had little more than a few days left to inhabit his body. Their journey continued until they arrived in the jungle country of Kusinara, where they rested in a grove of *sala* trees. This is where Buddha would meet his last disciple.

Hearing that the Buddha was nearby, a wandering monk named Subhadda rushed to the grove in the hope of meeting the master. Ananda stopped him. 'The Lord is weary,' he cautioned Subhadda. 'Do not trouble him.'

The Buddha had overheard the conversation. 'Let him in, Ananda,' he said. 'He is an earnest spiritual inquirer.'

Subhadda, who had practised under many famous spiritual teachers of the time, asked the Buddha, 'What do you think of all these venerated teachers? Are their teachings correct?'

'Do not trouble yourself as to whether they are right or wrong,' said Buddha. 'I shall teach you the true doctrine.' And so the Buddha then gave his very last advice to his very last disciple.

'What is important is the eightfold path, for only by following that path can a person become a true saint. If a teacher teaches that eightfold path then true enlightenment will follow; if the path is absent, so too will enlightenment be absent.'

Subhadda then left, and the Buddha turned to Ananda. 'It may be, Ananda,' he said, 'that people will say that without the Buddha, the great teacher, there will be no teacher. You should not think in this way. It is the lessons and disciplines that I have taught which should be your teacher when I am gone.'

Lord Buddha's time was drawing near, and he addressed his monks, the *bhikkus*, one last time. 'If any of you still have any doubts about the Buddha and the teaching, you should ask me now, so that you will have no cause to regret that you did not ask me while I was still with you.'

None of the monks said anything. None had any questions. All were silent.

The Buddha said, 'Perhaps it is out of respect for your teacher that you do not question me. Still the monks remained silent.

Eventually Ananda rose to his feet. 'My Lord,' he said to Buddha, 'I believe that in this great company of monks there is not one who has a single doubt or question about the Buddha and his teachings.'

Then the Buddha looked one last time around the assembled *bhikkus*. 'O monks,' he said, 'this is my very last advice to you. *Vaya dhamma sankhara, appamadena sampadetha.* Every single thing in the world is changeable. Nothing lasts for ever. Each of you must work hard to gain your own salvation.'

These were the Buddha's very last words.

He lay back on the couch among the *sala* trees in the lion posture, on his right side with both legs stretched, his left hand resting on his left thigh and his right hand supporting his head.

Word had already spread far and wide that Lord Buddha was about to pass away, and devotees started pouring into the clearing in an unending stream. The word of his passing reached heaven, and the gods assembled in the sky above.

The Most Enlightened One then lay still, closed his eyes, and journeyed through all the levels of consciousness. It was a spiritual journey that the Buddha alone could undertake, into the realm of ultimate reality.

TAKING THINGS FURTHER

The real read

This *Real Reads* volume of *Siddhartha Gautama: The Life of the Buddha* is our interpretation of the events in the life of the founder of the great religion of Buddhism.

After the Buddha died, his teachings were written down from what people remembered, though it is important to recognise that this was often many years after the Buddha's death, and until they were written down many of the stories were handed down by teachers remembering what they had heard and retelling them to their pupils.

This means that there are often several versions of each part of the story of Buddha's life, and even more versions of his teachings. One of the main sources for the life and teachings of the Buddha is the Pali Canon or Tripitaka, which means the 'three baskets of teaching'; this is a collection of Buddha's sayings, his thoughts about them, and rules for Buddhist monks.

Back in time

When Siddhartha was born in northern India in 566 BCE, the region was divided into different states. Some, like the Vrji Republic, were ruled by public assemblies and democratic institutions; others, like the kingdoms of Kosala and Magadha, were ruled by a monarch; yet others, like Sakya, were ruled by kings who were elected. All states, however, functioned within the structure of Brahminism, which defined the duties of a ruler rather than the means of governing. Siddhartha was born in Sakya, a republic with an elected monarch; Sakya was later incorporated into the kingdom of Kosala.

At the time when Siddhartha was growing up, a major change was taking place in the way wealth and power were distributed. Money was taking the place of cattle and crops as a way of measuring wealth, and cities and their markets were growing quickly. Merchants managed to accumulate great fortunes, and in some cases became wealthier than the kings.

The kings fought back by passing laws to control commerce and trade. With their emphasis on money and the use of force to maintain ever stricter rules, the kingdoms soon became more powerful than the republics – economically, politically and militarily. As a result, many people felt that their freedom was becoming increasingly more restricted, and their suffering and hardship ever greater. Many philosophers and teachers of the time, including Buddha, sought liberation through spiritual rather than political means.

These teachers of spiritual liberation and their followers tended to follow one of two traditions. Some, whose members came exclusively from the brahmin caste, embraced the principles of working within society to bring about change. They worshipped fire, chanted from the Hindu scriptures or *vedas*, bathed in rivers to wash away their sins, and worshipped the one supreme god Brahma, union with whom was considered the goal of spiritual life.

Others, whose leaders and followers came from castes other than the brahmin, believed that it was essential to leave society altogether in order to seek ultimate truth. They often lived in the forest as a spiritual community or *sangha*, and believed that people should not be judged according to their caste. These groups and their leaders rejected the idea of one supreme god or creator, believing instead in the interconnectedness and cyclical nature of the universe. This was the route that Buddha and his followers took and developed into Buddhism.

Major places and festivals

There are four major places of pilgrimage in Buddhism:

- Lumbini, near Kapilavastu, where Siddhartha was born;

- Bodh Gaya, where he attained enlightenment;

- Sarnath, where he preached his first sermon;

- Kusinagar, where he passed away.

Other important places associated with the Buddha include:

- Jetavana near Sravasti, where the Buddha spent twenty-five years towards the end of his life.

- Sanchi, near Bhopal in Madhya Pradesh, where the Buddha's relics as well as those of Sariputta and Mahamoggallana are enshrined.

- Rajgir and the surrounding area, especially the Gridhra-kuta mountain, where Buddha rested when preaching.

- The Ajanta Caves in Maharashtra, an important pilgrim and tourist attraction, famous for its many paintings and sculptures on Buddhist themes.

The main Buddhist festival is Vaisakha Purnima, the full moon day in the late spring month of Vaisakha. This is considered a thrice-blessed day in the Buddhist calendar, because it was the day that the Buddha was born, the day he attained enlightenment, and the day he passed into *nirvana*.

Finding out more

We recommend the following books and websites to gain a better and greater understanding of the Buddha.

Books

- Jonathan Landaw and Janet Brooke, *Prince Siddhartha: The Story of Buddha*, Wisdom, 2011.

- Narada Mahathera, *The Buddha and His Teachings*, Wisdom, 1998.

- Walpola Rahula, *What the Buddha Thought*, Grove Press, 1974.

- Edwin Arnold, *Light of Asia*, Book Jungle, 2006.

Websites

- www.bbc.co.uk/religion/religions/buddhism/
The BBC's excellent web page on Buddhism.

- www.ancientindia.co.uk/buddha/
home_set.html
A website about the Buddha, his life and his teachings.

- www.buddhanet.net/e-learning/
basic-guide.htm
An excellent introduction to Buddhist history and ideas.

- www.pbs.org/thebuddha/
An online version of the documentary about the Buddha's life made by the award-winning filmmaker David Grubin.

Food for thought

The life and teachings of the Buddha have inspired many teachers and scholars, and been the source of thousands of books. There are so many interpretations and versions of Buddhism that it would be impossible to list them all. You could spend many years learning about the differences between the main Theravada and Mahayana schools of Buddhism, then even more years finding out about Tibetan Buddhism, Japanese Shingon and Tendai, Zen Yoga, and many many more.

This small book is only the tip of the iceberg, just a taste of the wonderful world of Buddhist literature. Reading more about the Buddha and his ideas will always reward you with interesting stories, great characters, and important ideas.

Here are some things to think about if you are reading the story of Siddhartha Gautama alone, and some ideas for discussion if you are reading it with friends.

Starting points

- Do you think Siddhartha was right to leave his wife and child and go in search of enlightenment?

- What do you think of King Suddhodana's plan to keep Siddhartha from finding out about the pain and suffering in the world outside the palace gates? Is it a good idea to protect children from seeing pain and suffering in others?

- Which event in the book did you find the most interesting and intriguing? What particularly appeals to you about it?

- Find some words and phrases in the story that you find difficult to understand. Research their meanings and try writing your own definitions of them.

Group activities

- Siddhartha sat and meditated for many hours at a time in order to understand what life is about. Talk with your group about what each of you thinks meditation is, and what it is useful for. You might like to try meditating as a group; one way to do this is to sit on cushions in a circle with a vase of flowers or a beautiful stone in the centre to concentrate on. You can find many practical ideas about how to approach meditation on the internet at www.buddhamind. info/leftside/sumaries/activity.htm

- Choose one of the group to roleplay Buddha, and ask that person to explain one of the important ideas of Buddhism to the rest of the group, who are the disciples. The disciples can ask questions.

- In your group, imagine what would happen if Buddha were to return today. What sort of examples might he give to illustrate the eightfold path?